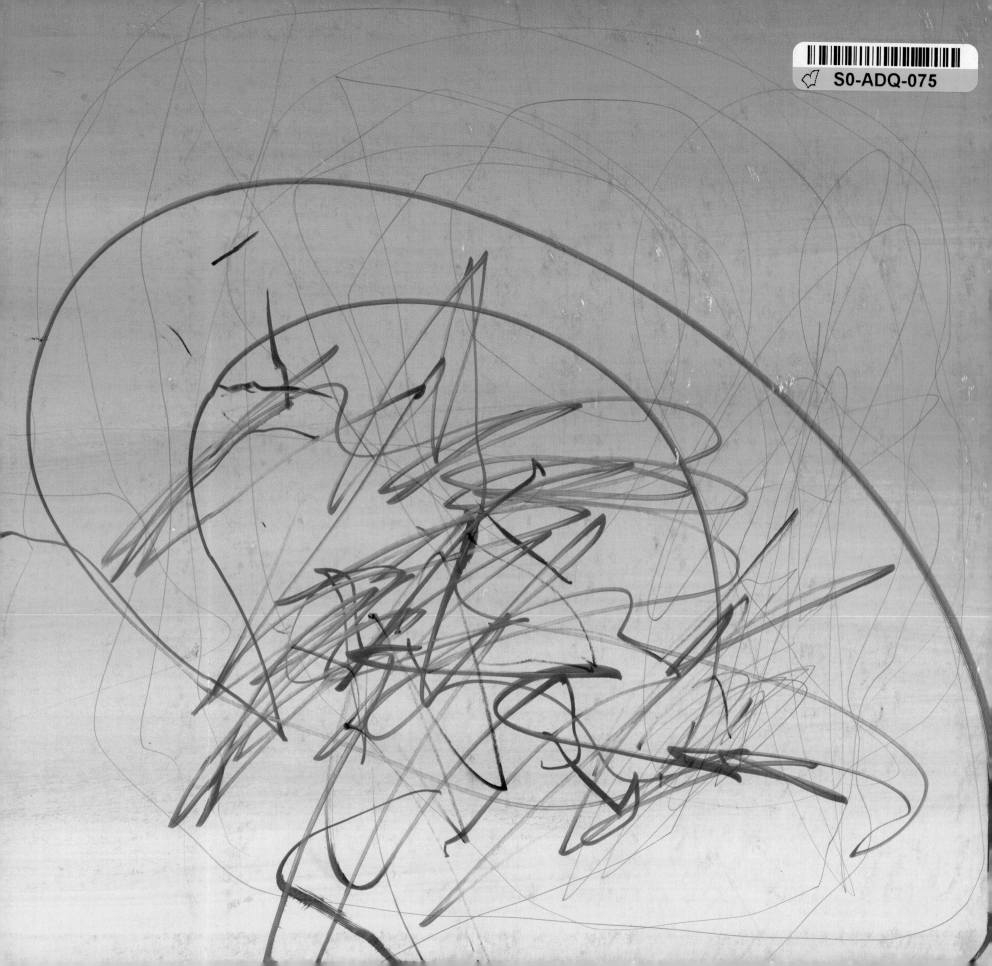

For Marcel – *IvdH*

For Thomas – *MtC*

Library of Congress Cataloging-in-Publication Data is available.

LEMNISCAAT
An Imprint of Boyds Mills Press, Inc.
A Highlights Company

815 Church Street
Honesdale, Pennsylvania 18431

A Strange Day

Iris van der Heide

ILLUSTRATIONS BY Marijke ten Cate

Lemniscaat

The wind is howling around Jack's house on the hill. The trees are swaying and Jack is restless. He wanders from the window to the door and from the door to the mailbox ... and back again.

"What's the matter?" his mother asks.

"Today is the day I find out if I won the drawing contest!" Jack says.

Jack hears a clatter and runs to the mailbox again.
Nothing! There is NOTHING in there! Except one postcard
from his aunt in Morocco. Why isn't there a letter for him?

With tears in his eyes, Jack walks through the park.
"So I didn't win," he thinks. "They could at least have
sent something. Just a short note, saying "'Dear Jack, we
really liked your drawing but you didn't win.'"

The wind is blowing through Jack's hair. He doesn't
feel it. He doesn't even notice when he stops the
runaway baby stroller.

"I did draw a beautiful castle, right?
And nice knights? Don't they like castles
and knights?" Jack mumbles.

The children are shouting. Without
thinking, Jack blocks the ball.

"Didn't I do everything right to win?" Jack thinks.
"I even bought a silver marker to color the knights."

The birds are chirping. Jack doesn't hear them.

"I will never enter a drawing contest again!" Jack says. Suddenly a small dog lands in Jack's arms. Two bikes have crashed right behind him. Jack barely notices and quickly puts the dog down on the sidewalk.

Sadly, Jack strolls home.

When Jack gets to his mailbox, he sees
something white sticking out. "What's that?"
He quickly opens the big envelope.

Dear Jack,

Congratulations! You have won the
drawing contest. Your beautiful castle and
silver knights are superb!

Sincerely,
The Judges

"I won, I won after all!" Jack shouts. He dances up the sidewalk.

A crowd is gathered in front of Jack's house on the hill. Some people cheer and clap, others point at him. One person has even brought flowers.

Jack is surprised. How do they know he has won?

"We want to thank you for what you did,"
the woman with the flowers says.

"Did you like it?" Jack asks proudly.

"You saved my baby!" the woman replies.

Jack looks at her in amazement.

"You helped us win the soccer
match!" the group of children shouts.

"And you saved the egg that was falling from
the tree," a girl says, giving Jack a kiss.
Jack blushes.

"And you saved my dog!"
the old man says. "Thank you!"

"Well, you are all welcome!"
Jack says at last.

Later that day Jack sits at his favorite spot. He smiles
while he looks out over the fields. What a strange day!